WIND OF WONDER

*An Eclectic Collection
of Short Stories*

By

Maria D. Lopez Berna

Copyright © 2023 Maria D. Lopez Berna.

All rights reserved. No part of this publication may be reproduced, distributed, or transmitted in any form or by any means, including photocopying, recording, or other electronic or mechanical methods, without the prior written permission of the publisher, except in the case of brief quotations embodied in critical reviews and certain other non-commercial uses permitted by copyright law.

Names, characters, and places are products of the author's imagination.

Front cover image by Ritiele Ramonica.

Book design by Hamza.

m.d.lopez.berna@gmail.com

Table of Contents

An Old Favourite Song	1
Christmas Spirit	5
My Secrets Are Mine	10
Fairy Tale	14
A Couple of Surprises	18
Grey Bridge Town	22
Shattered	29
The Love Letter I Never Wrote...	34
Devoted Strangers	38
Acknowledgements	40
About the Author	42

An Old Favourite Song

I smile, a nervous, unsteady smile on my face that my lips fight to maintain. Like it has been badly drawn on a lousy clown's face. It perfectly coordinates with the rest of my trembling body, unable to settle as I walk along the squeaking wooden floor of the excessively flowery aisle, like a dancer performing the wrong song. My anxious eyes struggle to look up where the towering figure awaits, at the end of the narrow path which tightens with every step I take. It leads me ahead, confirming my route, only advancing my steps forward with no option to return. The stifling path has no space for air, as though I am inside a sealed box. My heavy feet move closer and closer, and the rest of my body follows, like a dog on a leash.

I am happy. Yes! I am. This is the best day of my life. I am happy. Yes. Yes, I am!

I keep on repeating, like a song learnt by heart that replays in my head.

I shrink. I fade. With zero control of my own body, the zombie in white proceeds. All eyes are on me, on the protagonist, the sleepwalker of this blurred dream. Face forward, evading the intense gazes of the expectant spectators of this show, I continue to move. But I can still feel them all, like stabs on my skin: the piercing eyes, the happy hum, the compliments, the attention, the judgment. Like a criminal walking sluggishly into the courtroom to hear her verdict - A life sentence.

On the happiest day of my life, here I am.

I reach the end of the path. A void of air. One final step to where two figures are standing. Three, now with myself included. Two of them are present and one is absent. Only one speaks, but my anxiety prevents me from hearing. The voice is an echo, an unsettling disturbance that amplifies in my head.

It seems like a different lifetime ago when I needed to move on and learn to live a life of emptiness. Everyone insisted on taking me out and seeing me happy, and I tried; I was so damn good at pretending that they believed it. It became my full-time job. Even I believed it. I learnt to use a mask of joy and bandages covering the painful wounds, keeping them out of sight, hoping that if they can't be seen they can't exist.

Then John came along wearing his persuasive smile and bringing a glint of hope to my path of sorrow. I let him in, following an illusion. A light that was born on a much-insisted blind date. He was able to offer a distraction to my restless heart. My life found some peace and conformity but sometimes I was so lost in my memories that a song came back to play in my head. A long-loved catchy melody.

John waited persistently. He was my present, my future, but not my past. The events that unfolded just followed a natural progression and I couldn't stop any of it. John seized the occasion when I was yearning for love, by going down on one knee and letting the world witness. An audience by design meticulously created. Excitement and interest arose from both worlds. Who was I to reject everyone's happiness? As for mine, I couldn't tell.

The months that followed were like a poster ad, a picture of impeccable smiles and matchless eyes with the expression of a doll. The nights were filled with the required romantic dates, rehearsing for the big performance. Meanwhile, I was learning a new song, which I played repeatedly in my head in a failed attempt to replace an old favourite. The one, which of late, frequently infiltrated and played loudly in my head. I secretly let it play and honestly, I enjoyed it. It took me back to my old life, to feelings, to myself…

Back to my criminal trial. My eyes are still lost, perhaps too excited to focus:

Because I'm happy, yes, I am! The song keeps playing, trying to keep the catchy old one out.

In an instant, there is no more noise. Now the cacophony has become a voice crystal clear. "If anyone has an objection to why this man and this woman should not be wed, speak now or forever hold your peace."

A spark is lit. The sleepwalker awakes. A distinctive excitement is rising in me. A sound rises from behind me.

Someone moving. *Could it be?*

Suddenly a bright voice sounds like a much-loved song in the most unexpected and inappropriate place. Although for me the most loved and expected song, an all-time favourite.

"I object!"

I turn to find his reassuring face among the alarmed witnesses. Standing. Outstanding. Stunning. The only visible face in a blurred crowd.

Relieved, I Smile.

CHRISTMAS SPIRIT

Three days until Christmas, an unusual one. A different location this time, a colder and more distant Christmas. And yes, a much-expected white one. Jonas was a fearful and timid city boy. He did not enjoy the idea of spending Christmas in an isolated countryside house, even with the additional appeal of probable snowfall. It was a house that had been in the family for generations. His mum's childhood and his mum's dad's. A typical antique granny house, with its old wooden smell of the floor and furniture. Storage of entire lives. There was history impregnated in those walls, preserved stories, some never told, some forgotten, but the essence remained.

Jonas and his parents were meeting the rest of his family, to spend what was likely to be his grandmother's last Christmas. The adults' loudest secret. The whole family arrived, and the silence was disrupted. His cousins were either too old or too young to give any attention to Jonas or vice versa.

Therefore, Jonas chose to spend his time outside, playing with a blonde boy called Patrick, whom he had previously found hovering around the backside of the country house, that stretched far and wide into the deep forest.

The curious boy was very interested in Jonas' family and listened to everything Jonas said. Jonas was a loner, but this time he appreciated the company of his new friend. He enjoyed the connection they shared and felt like they'd known each other for years. With him, Jonas felt confident and understood. Every morning Jonas rushed through his breakfast to go outside and play. Then he'd come back at lunch, like a hungry puppy led by the aroma of homemade food. His mum insisted on spending some quality family time inside and even though he accepted and enjoyed the warmth, he couldn't stop looking at the powerful wooden clock on the living room wall, ticking as loud as the family's festive chatter. When his mum finally allowed him, Jonas would run to find his new friend, who was always waiting, no matter how late Jonas was.

That evening the air was starting to become icier, and when they spoke, misty clouds escaped with every word.

On that same Christmas Eve, right before the snowfall, the boy seemed quieter than usual. Jonas had presumed the boy had something going on at home as he never mentioned his family. Jonas had imagined that perhaps Patrick liked to hear stories about the family he wished to have, and for this reason, Jonas never asked.

"It's getting colder Jonas, I think it's going to snow any time soon, you should go back home. We should go home."

"I have never seen the snow," answered Jonas searching for a snowflake in the sky with squinted eyes. "You're right, we should go... our mums will be worried sick. It's Christmas tomorrow!" he added with contagious excitement, a sudden luminosity grew on his face like a lightbulb had been lit by the mere thought.

Before parting their ways, the boy lifted his bowed head and look at Jonas saddened. "I heard your grandmother is very ill," he whispered, uncertain of Jonas' reaction.

"Yes, unfortunately," Jonas replied, avoiding the boy's gaze.

"Make sure you hug her and tell her how much you love her, and not to fear, she will soon join her husband," said the boy sounding more confident this time.

Jonas turned away to face home, embarrassed of exposing his watery eyes.

"Jonas!" the boy called before Jonas could move his feet.

"You know in these old houses it's easy to lose things in between the gaps of the floorboards... if something drops in, you may never see it if you don't purposely search for it. Things like jewellery... rings. A ring can easily roll and get stuck in those gaps, believe me, you should check it out..."

Jonas listened to the senseless advice while nodding and gazing with his pensive eyes before turning.

Jonas arrived at the house. The rest were all gathered in the living room. But the recent words of the blonde boy had followed him home. To dry his teary eyes, he sat with his thoughts in the old and dusty sitting room, when an old, blurry black-and-white picture of a familiar face, caught his eye. A blonde boy. Mum came in looking for him.

"Mum, who is he?" Jonas asked as his mum held the picture in her hands for a closer inspection. A warm smile surfaced on her face as her eyes softened.

"Your grandfather was adorable when he was a child," she said.

Jonas' muscles froze. Heaviness dropped into his core. His chest tightened, squeezing his heart. His flat gaze rewound the last few days like in a film, with the hazy images flashing past as his dizzy head tried to remember. When his body was able to respond after a long period of numbness, his confused mum followed him while he searched with determination the old rusty floor in each room.

Finally, under his grandmother's bed, where she was peacefully asleep, Jonas found an antique shiny but modest engagement ring with a scratched stone that had seen better days. Jonas looked at his grandmother and after a second of doubt, he woke her up. At the presence of the piece of jewellery, the misty eyes of the dedicated lady filled with sparks. Her lip lines stretched, drawing the cheerfulness found in a child's honest smile. Witnessing such pure happiness in her eyes, Jonas finally allowed his confined tears to run freely down his face.

"How? Where? I thought I lost it; I thought I would never ... Patrick... I asked my Patrick every night to help me find it... I couldn't go... w..." her vulnerable broken voice was unable to continue.

Jonas, quite speechless, gave her a sincere hug while his mum watched, holding a ball of emotions from the bedroom door. And it was at that precise moment that the first snowflake descended slowly from the cold cloudy sky. Delicate and light as a tiny piece of cotton, continued its journey gently and free, marking the beginning of a long and anticipated snowy night.

MY SECRETS ARE MINE

Steps approaching. My room is as black as coal. The streetlight had blown out. My tone low but agitated, keeps on calling the other person in the room. I don't know his name, I don't remember if he ever told me, I can't recall seeing him before. No response. I try again and again. It's too late for him now... *is it late for me too?* My eyes are sore. My eyelids are like loose thick blinds that I can no longer hold up, I try but... fatigue wins.

The day goes by as normal as it can go. *What is normal anymore?* Every day is like watching a scene in a movie, where everything has been previously rehearsed. But I am not watching from my couch; I am a part of this farce. With kind smiles and caring words, they think they can deceive me. I search in their eyes for a hint of truth, for stolen secrets, a lapse in a moment of carelessness, or a slip of their tongue. Nobody can pretend for that long. *Fools!*

When the daylight dies, fear consumes me. Those steps…I know what they do, I know they will come back. *Don't sleep… don't sleep…* then darkness arrives.

Insipid food on my plate, I place the spoon in my mouth out of force of habit. Meanwhile, I secretly listen to the bland people and their silence, or the occasional idiotic conversations, yet always on alert for a clue.

"Will you eat that and be quiet? I am trying to eat in peace."

"Let the man tell his jokes."

"They aren't funny."

"Do you know what is funny George? Your trumps."

The table bursts with laughter.

"That is true I heard his farts from my room. What did you eat George?

The teasing continues…

"Talking about last night, I heard Mr Rowen sharing secrets with Ms Steven right before I headed to my room, I saw them whispering in each other's ears. Then I heard them from my bed, they wouldn't shut up. Until Ms Steven said Shh! Not now, when they are asleep."

"Yes, the night before they were murmuring about some mistake... I remember I was trying to stay awake, waiting for Andrew, but he never came back, I haven't seen him since..."

Tonight, is not as dark; a dim yellow streetlight outside my window, fixed at last. The street noise fades away. My companion, my heartbeat. I wait silently. I won't sleep. They want me to; they need me to. They come in at night, I am certain, I have heard them, everyone has. They want our secrets, they need them, but I won't let them. They think I will close my eyes, but I will be ready. The other person in the room is fast asleep, it may also be too late for the others. The waiting may be long, but I can do it, I will hold my eyelids open. Tonight, is different, I feel stronger.

I feel them. Steps slowly approaching. My heart beats faster, my breathing is louder, and the night is still silent. Now I hear them closer, the whispers, the hisses, the movement outside my door, steps everywhere! *Not this time, I'm ready!* I reach for the knife under my pillow and storm out the door. *I bet the fools did not expect that.* I stab and stab the darkness. I run, pushing my way through. I race downstairs. I hear them all now, all around me. I throw chairs, my targets keep moving. Louder voices behind me. I am cornered. My bloody knife is stolen from my hand in a second of weakness, seized and pushed down forcefully, I fight back up, but I can't. I lost my battle. A sharp stab in my neck. *No!* I'm defeated...

"Why didn't he take his sleeping pills?" yelled a heated voice amongst screams and weeps.

"I gave them to him last night, I saw him taking them doctor," answered the terrified nurse.

"Well, clearly, he didn't. Now with that amount of tranquillizer that we injected in his neck, he won't be waking up tonight. Please take him to his room. And how the hell did he get a knife? No one goes anywhere, we have a lot of explaining to do when the police arrive."

Fairy Tale

New threat. A note from Tyler. Again. But not as terrifying as last week's one. If he truly intended to harm me, he would have already done it years ago. I was frightened at first when the notes came anonymously. Then he exposed himself by signing them, making a fool of himself, just like he always did when we were kids at school. Pathetic! Will he ever stop?

I ignore it. Again. I am walking on air right now; nothing will affect me. James and I are celebrating five delightful months together and I won't let this unfortunate individual ruin it for us. This is my fairy tale.

I was 13, back to school on a blue Monday. Before the weekend, my mum had forced me to get that ridiculous haircut that I despised so much. I adored my long hair, most of the popular girls had long hair. I saw the way they were desired; I just had been deprived of that power by a pair of scissors.

It had been my dad's birthday that weekend, my face had burnt with the thought of going to that house. I yearned for those days when it was just the two of us. When I did not have to compete for his attention with a smaller version of me, both cuter and smarter. Before the match, her name was already written on the trophy-my dad. I was always a visitor in her fortress. The defender, who kept on committing penalties and her goals were painfully scored every time. I could do nothing but observe her victory sullenly and feel the effect of keeping my teeth clenched over the weekend in the form of a sore jaw.

Cloudy blue Monday with traces of the weekend in my memory, and then -Thomas... a face that makes you dream. My face blushed. A group of boys and girls were with him blocking the main door. The air was thick. Tyler's sweaty chubby cheeks appeared in the crowd, rushing with a paper in his hand and clumsily bumped into me. The empathy shown on my face rapidly washed away as soon as I heard the mockery and laughter. On the asphalt, I spotted my way out, my salvation from an inevitable humiliation, an opportunity to level up while pushing him lower, and I did not hesitate. I was powerful... and Thomas was watching, everybody was. I picked up the note and read out the secrets written on that piece of paper. The only time, I dared to look at his face, it was about to set on fire. I doubted if he could see me through the thick white fog covering his glasses. It was a love note, directed to myself, which I did not anticipate.

Would I have read it, had I known? Most probably not, but it was too late, I had to endure the bully I became.

I pushed away any feelings of pity every time I looked at him in the days to come, through an emotionless protector screen that my eyes created and I ensured to never remove. Since that day, I regained the power that I had once felt I lost due to my stupid hair.

After a 3-hour drive, we are finally at the wooden cabin. It's October and the autumn leaves create a beautiful orange carpet, setting the most perfect mood, the picture-perfect setting for my tale. We've known each other for a few months, but it feels as if I've always known him. I feel our chemistry is so powerful that I can physically see the sparks when our bodies are near. We wake up in this charming rustic cabin the next day, after the most wonderful night, the perfect couple date, in my fairy tale. Today we are going for a hike. I feel uncertain about this, but James has a surprise for me.

After a draining hour in the isolated woods, we come across a difficult path on a steep hill. Hands hold tight. James stops, leaves his backpack on the ground, and with a map in hand moves ahead to accidentally step on a loose root. He stumbles down, holding on to a fragile root while searching for my arm, and I watch him fall until silence appears.

About to collapse and with a cold body, I reach the cabin tearfully, squeezing his backpack in my arms. I find his wallet on the table; his driving licence is peeking from the side. Without thinking, I pick it up with my shaky hand, my moist and unfocused eyes staring at his picture, my tears blocking my sight.

Next to his face, his name, *Tyler Smith*. I wipe my eyes to read it again. My heart stops... My mind goes back to James' young face, chubby cheeks, and foggy glasses. The far-lost memory surfaces back, now crystal clear. Confused, I search in his backpack; A rope, a knife, a journal with screams of hatred, and a picture of my face purposely scratched. The ending in James' fairy tale.

A Couple of Surprises

"What is this mum?" said Amber coughing the dust away.

"Let me see," said her mum, swiping the dust in the air with her left hand, while opening a big worn cardboard box. Mother and daughter covered their nose and mouth while looking among the filthy ancient books inside the large box.

"Wow, mum what are these? They look like papers... Are they papers mum? How old are they?" asked the excited little girl.

"Very old Amber, I couldn't say. Yes, they are, they look like pieces of paper with words on them."

"Words?" said Amber amazed, gently passing her finger over the printed words, as if she was reading in braille. Her eyes were shining so bright with such discovery, that they could lighten the old, dark attic.

"I think these are what they used to call books," said Amber's mum hesitant, looking around at all the old filthy boxes lying around, wondering how long they had been hidden in her grandparents' attic and where else they had been. Her excited eyes filled up with the anticipation of what else was to be unboxed.

What once had been a colourful book caught the little girl's attention. Despite the faded material, the colours and pictures were slightly visible. A boy and a toddler were happily playing on the book cover. "My little Brother", read the intrigued girl, word by word. "Mum! What is a brother?" Her mum looked at the girl puzzled, bereft of an apt answer. She shrugged her shoulders and shook her doubtful head while skimming the room. "I don't know love, but we will find the answers to all those questions."

30 years later...

"This may feel cold," warned Amber with a comforting smile.

The scan room was filled with the excitement of a thrilled couple prepared to see their child for the very first time. Routine questions were asked, and the loving couple responded with anxious smiles and shared understanding. Unexpectedly, the midwife froze. Silence invaded the room. Uncertainty and concern arose among the impatient couple.

"What is it?" asked Tom distressed, as the frozen doctor was gazing at the screen.

Silence.

"What is wrong?" demanded the uneased mother.

"Two... two babies," whispered Amber after a prolonged pause.

The puzzled couple looked at each other.

The midwife glanced at the door and spoke as though telling a secret, "I don't know how this happened ...I read about this but never saw any proof... You are having two babies." Her eyes filled with excitement, as though her lifelong questions had been answered.

"What?" cried Jenny alarmed.

"Yes, I understand it was normal, having more than one child and the ones born together were called twins. You are having twins!" she explained looking at the confused and terrified faces.

"How is this possible?" her voice trembling; "Will the child have two bodies? I don't understand. Is there a cure?"

The midwife continued; "They are two different babies, with their different brains and personalities." Amber tried her very best to keep her lips from forming a smile. "This is extraordinary! Those scientists and doctors that believed it, weren't crazy after all! Sadly, they were all erased together with the existing documents back in the late 2800s. They were convinced that vaccines were created to secure our future on the overpopulated planet. Some books could be saved, and I was lucky to have some in my possession... Books were reams of papers with words on them," she added after watching the sceptical faces of the couple. "Some would tell stories, and some had information. But this! This is finally proof that everything was real!" said Amber trying to tone down her enthusiasm.

The petrified and perplexed couple was lost for words.

"Do not fear," said Amber; "I will take care of the delivery. Fortunately, you are having identical twins, and no one will know, because, in the eyes of the world, you'll have only one child."

Grey Bridge Town

"Imagine there was a lake with water so enchanted and pure that would wash away all of your sins," said the odd-looking woman.

The two girls shared looks of mischief.

"And where is this lake?" Sandra responded.

"Only those who've truly sinned can be bathed."

The girls laughed and parted mocking the lady.

There were several rumours and gossip in the town, and it all led to the same conclusion for the people who lived there. She was a witch. Only a few pitied her, convinced that she was just a poor scruffy old lady, whose hard life reflected in her physical condition. She was avoided by the parents and taunted by the children, although they quivered anytime, she was near.

Sandra was becoming weary of hearing the same tales every time her parents took her to the small town to visit her grandparents. Grey Bridge Town was an old and drained town lost on the other side of the woods, where it felt like you had gone 50 years back in time. This time she brought company, her friend Camila, who even though already had heard some of the stories from her friend, and had seen the witch herself, was fascinated and eager to learn more about her.

"She is always alone with her cat," said the youngest boy with wide-open eyes, leaning forward, trying to add something to the older children's stories.

"She doesn't have any cats!" said his brother.

"She is a witch!"

"So?" asked his big brother narrowing his eyes. "She doesn't have any cats; we've never seen one."

"So, how do you know? Because you've never seen them, doesn't mean she doesn't have them. All witches have cats..." said the boy in a quieter voice as though suddenly realising that his words could travel through the silence of the night.

Another girl continued, interrupting, and adding to the enthusiasm on the faces. "My cousin told me that his granny told him, that the witch had lived in Grey Bridge Town years ago and one day she vanished. No one heard from her for like 40 years and her house was empty. No one dared to get close. One day she came back looking like the same age, but her face seemed different, like a different person or something."

The pupils of the children's eyes were becoming wider with every tale, their muscles were tightening, and their legs weakening. Everyone was trying to disguise the almost tangible fear.

"My aunt told me that once the witch was in her friend's dream, and when she woke up, she was outside her window".

"Wow, I've got goosebumps," said a boy while rubbing his arms. Everyone smirked sharing thrilled looks which showed mutual understanding.

"She goes out at night to collect things for her potions like dead rats and that sort of things and she always talks about a lake and sins."

"Sins? She doesn't go to church, does she? She is a witch; they just do witchcraft and stuff."

Every child was adding their version of the story they had heard, and the tension was growing so intensely that they could jump with terror at a simple creak of a twig. Camila kept discreetly looking behind her shoulder.

"And what is her name?" she asked.

All the children simultaneously shrugged their shoulders and pressed their lips, looking at each other's faces for the answer. Suddenly a loud meow came from the woods. The children's faces turned pale, as though the colour in their faces had been washed out. They ran clumsily for their lives, with screams of horror.

"See? The witch's cat!" cried out the young boy, almost out of breath.

Camila never forgot the tales she heard in Grey Bridge town; she always shared them whenever she intended to set a spooky mood. Years passed and so did, the sweet innocence of childhood and the irresponsible joy of adolescence, giving way to the reality of adulthood, when one must face accountability for their actions.

Camila had become a young woman; stuck in an unhappy marriage. She believed her husband had an affair and even though she loved him with all her heart, deluded by suspicion, she sought revenge. One long night out after a hard day at work, alcohol and resentment got the best of her. It ended up with the beginning of a new life growing inside her. No one knew her secret.

Then came the night when everything would change. She had mentally prepared herself to face her most terrible fear. The face of the person who had made her miserable and ruined her marriage was finally going to be revealed. The waiting time at the restaurant table, pretending to be calm in front of her husband, felt like an eternity.

Meanwhile, a hundred hands were pressing her chest emptying her lungs, slowly deflating it. She could not anticipate her own reaction, after meeting the reason for so many restless nights at last. Then she came in through the restaurant's door, holding hands with her wife.

She was stunning, she had light ginger hair, the same type she had seen on the passenger seat of her husband's car. She was wearing a big, relaxed smile, the one that shows sincerity, the one that hides no secrets. She looked very much in love with the other woman, the kind of love that one cannot pretend, the couple left a trail of truth as they passed.

There was not enough time for all the work stories they could share. Camila thoroughly searched the woman's eyes in all the instances their eyes met, but there were no secrets hidden there. It had all been a big misunderstanding. They had just been great work partners, steadily moving up the career ladder. But she was not relieved, a much heavier feeling started to squeeze her chest tighter than it had ever before. The loud voices in the busy restaurant became muffled and distant. Then, loud, and clear, the sound of a tiny heartbeat, the reminder of her sin.

Nothing seemed to have changed in Grey Bridge Town. She wondered if any of the people she crossed by were children from that night; if there was any new story to tell. She couldn't recognise anyone, but the old, spine-chilling house, the one she once feared. Without hesitation, she knocked. A large squeaking wooden door revealed the figure of the old lady, looking intently into her eyes, Camila's heart shrank.

"You mentioned a magic lake a long time ago, I need it to be true, please tell me it is real," cried Camila with despair.

After a long pause and a rapid shift of expression in her eyes, the wrinkled woman spoke, "Follow me."

Long was the way but returning home was not an option to consider anymore and she eagerly followed the slow footsteps of the woman.

"Are you really a witch?"

No response.

After a tiring and solitary walk, a modest and timid lake opened to sight. The woman halted and looked fixedly at the mysterious dark waters before their eyes. It was different from Camila's expectations. Nothing like the magical and mystical lake she had anticipated. Uneased, she waited for the old woman to speak. Still no words. Quivering lips, there was no going back. A wave of uncertainty ran through her body like lightning. The old lady gave her an encouraging smile. She gulped and as if given a subtle push, she slowly and carefully entered the lake as though walking over spears. Her skin was pierced by the icy water and before an anguished scream could escape her mouth, there was a touch of a sudden warmth. The sky turned purplish. The stars vanished. Peace invaded and slowly consumed her. Outside once covered in wrinkles was now the resemblance of a young, dry Camila.

"Thank you," she muttered with a grim smile on her new acquired face. She turned back and headed for the sinful unwanted life. Sometimes what is refused by some can be desired by others.

SHATTERED

Early morning, I find myself on the couch. The living room is upside down again. I start to sweep the glass pieces before my sons get up, but before I can finish, my youngest lingers on the stairs with a frightened face.

"Don't you worry my dear, come downstairs, this time wasn't that bad." We both tidy up the mess in silence. I head to my eldest's bedroom door. His eyes fixed on the ceiling. No words. Not many lately. He is scared; we all are.

Fear filled the house to replace the emptiness he left. Loneliness and emptiness consume my heart. Too painful to bear. It was not easy with him and it's even worse without him. Only If he would leave us alone… Stop coming in at night to show his rage. To terrify his children. To petrify me. Events that my mind decides to forget. I rely on my selective memory to help me go on with the day because my children need me to keep fighting.

The headmistress sighs heavily before she speaks, "The reason why I called you in today is because Lewis has been involved in a fight with two other children in his class. I have spoken to all the concerned parties, the two boys, the class children who witnessed and the teacher who was present when the incident occurred. Apparently, everyone agrees that your son started it."

"That's not true! He called me a loser first!" yells Lewis pounding his fist against the headmistress' table.

The headmistress grimaces.

"Lewis, stop that! Apologise to Mrs Hughes immediately!" Lewis shakes his flush face and darts to the door, slamming it behind him. Heavy stomping can still be heard from outside the headmistress' office. She closes her eyes tightly and opens them again to continue.

"As I was saying, they all assure me that Lewis lost his temper and pushed the boy towards the tabletop. After that, he fought another boy who was defending him. Miss Jonson who was the teacher in their science class, tried very hard to separate them both. However, he kept kicking Miss Jonson very aggressively, which left several bruises on her leg, and as for the boy, he had to be taken to A&E due to the injury to his back. We have no news about that yet."

She pauses as though to let it all sink in and after a long sigh, she continues, "As you could just see," she says pointing at the empty chair where Lewis had been seated. "He seems very agitated lately. According to his file, I understand that his father was abusive, and I can recognise a great amount of uncontrollable anger that he is unable to deal with. I also understand you are the only parent in the household, that his father left. Is this right Mrs Clifford?"

"That's right, he left 3 months ago and he is in the hands of justice...He used to lose his temper easily. The situation at home has been hard... you know? I think we... the kids still miss him."

"Of course, of course, he is their father after all... Have they had any type of contact since he left?"

"No, they haven't, no...." I omit the part when he comes home at night. That part I don't want my head to replay.

"I am going to apply for a counselling referral for Lewis, it will be helpful for his anger issues. This may take several weeks to be approved. As you can understand this incident and his actions on the school premises are unacceptable, therefore, I am obliged to adhere to the school policy and suspend Lewis for a week."

The only sound on the way home is his loud breathing, travelling fast through his flaring nostrils. He refuses to speak to me after learning he is grounded without any video games. From time to time, I observe through the rear-view mirror, his tight facial muscles, and his fixed flat gaze, while the trees flash past him outside the window.

The weekend has arrived, and we spend all day out, an attempt at entertainment that felt like forced fun. A couple of smiles. A few words. They are not the same kids as they used to be. Traumatised. Worried. Edgy. It kills me to see the unease in their eyes, the spark is gone, I keep seeking but only find empty stares. On the outside, in some instances, they seem like normal kids just doing what normal kids do. They even spend time with other children today while I let them be, quietly observing with nostalgia. Time to head home. All I wish is for them to be worn out in case he returns tonight.

A goodnight kiss "Don't be afraid, go to sleep, if he comes back, he won't do anything to you, I'll make sure honey." He remains quiet and barely looks me in the eye. "Sam...." I call.

He breaks the silence, "Mum... I don't want to sleep, I'm scared..."

"Do you want me to stay with you tonight?" I ask.

"No, please go to sleep mum, don't go downstairs, don't cry...just..." my youngest insists. "Just go to sleep please, promise." His concerned eyes stare into mine. What are they filled with? Terror, Pity, Or both? I cannot quite read them.

Both in bed and doors closed, just the silence remains in the house at night, and it's on painful and lonely nights like these when emotions emerge. The massive ball of fire burns. Flames inside me that desperately need a way out, like a volcano eruption with tears of sorrow. It aches how much I miss him.

When I open my eyes. I am not in bed. I broke my promise. My dry mouth feels glued. My body is boiling, my wet hands sustain my heavy head like holding a bowling ball. Red sweat covers my hands as well as the cracked glass bottle lying on the carpet floor. The living room is torn apart as badly as ever. The children stand still on the stairwell holding hands.

"Come here children." They slowly shake their serious frightened faces. Wide open penetrating eyes. "Don't fear your dad, he is not here anymore."

"No, he is not... he was not here... it's not him... who we are scared of mum," says my eldest son.

"Then who are you scared of honey?"

Sam looks at me hesitant as though grasping courage with his breath and squeezing his elder brother's hand, he murmurs, "You mum, it's you..."

The Love Letter I Never Wrote...

"I love you" she whispers. The warmth of those three words touches my cheek. The heat is sustained by the proximity of her lips. They are sincere. I do not doubt them. I used to question them. Now it seems like an eternity ago, when I scarcely heard them, when I longed for the sound of those three simple words. When I cried in silence because I missed them. Because I missed you. Because of my pride and arrogance. Because I took them, and you, for granted. Because I failed to appreciate you. I am blessed to hear them so much lately and I detest that it was my egotism that previously stopped them from being said. Now I wish the sound of those words never fades. And your lips, a tattooist's tool, will mark my cheek forever.

"Those flowers need to be watered or they will wilt," Mum's voice mixes with the beeps.

"Where is Richard? He is always late, why can't he ever be on time?" Dad's voice is heating up.

"He will be here." Mum is always so serene trying to keep peace.

"He has no respect for anybody, and you know I'm right."

Distant beeps and alarms slip through the swing and creaks of the door, gentle steps approaching. "Hello, everyone!" Richard whispers as if someone was asleep.

"Hello" mimics his wife.

"Finally!"

"Leave him alone," interrupts mum in a higher tone.

"Has the doctor been here already?" My old brother sounds preoccupied. "Where is Oliver?"

"Your brother is in the cafeteria, and will be back any minute, we're still waiting".

"Well, we're all here then... Hello, my dear, How you doing?"

"Hi, Richard. Hi, Molly. It's nice to see you," says my wife while her hand still feels warm over mine. The silent anxiety travels through the air, in people's voices, in the constant involuntary tapping of someone's foot or lip biting.

"Good morning," a husky voice breaks into the room and tension rises, my brother Oliver and his wife's hum follows it in.

"Is everyone here?"

"Yes, doctor we all are." I can feel Mum's raspy throat.

"The committee is waiting. Shall we?" Then, a sudden audible noise of body movements, babbles, beeps, and the creak of the door...

Moving words and sensory goodbyes, erratic breathings, snivels, and sobs, everyone gets their moment of privacy. And in between the eventual swings and creaks, the sounds of distant beeps and hum sneak in.

And finally, you, the last one. The gentle touch of your skin maddens all the receptors of mine. Your broken breath struggles to form words. Honey, trust me there is no more to say, forget those conversations that were left incomplete and anything that our mouths said but our hearts regret. I forgive everything, please forgive my mistakes too. All those times I made you cry; I know there were many things I could have said, but I walked away instead. Because I am a coward. Because I was ashamed of making you feel that way.

Now I wish I could give you all those hugs that I evaded and the love that I neglected. I always thought there was time for things to be fixed. I was wrong. I was very wrong. I wish I had left it all in written words, for you to know. I know what today is about, soon the plug will be pulled because I can't respond. I can just quietly and steadily listen from the hospital bed and wish that you could hear the love letter that I never wrote, because my screams are so desperately loud in my head that I want to believe you hear them.

Devoted Strangers

Lucy: Breathe in, breathe out, don't panic. The butterflies are having a blast. Doors open. Breath stops. Face in flames. His unique scent impregnates the train. Oh, new T-shirt! He looks perfect. If I could just tell him that... Oh! he looks my way, my heart tries to escape through my neck. I hope he didn't see that, oh my god! Was I staring? I wonder if he ever sees me... Two more stops and I must wait one whole day to see him again, I will be brave today. He stands, I follow, I am ready to speak. We both hold onto the bar focused on the doors slowly opening, our hands don't touch but I feel the warmth of his skin, and I don't want to let go of this moment. Now! Now! I lose my voice, and he heads in his direction, I head in mine, just as every day...

Marc: Keep calm. Doors open. I am in. As soon as I see her, I lose control of my trembling and clumsy body. I hope she doesn't notice it. I look away hiding the blush. Her reflection on the glass window, looking beautiful in yellow. I wish I could tell her, I will. Yes! Today! Oh! Was she looking? Of course, she was! She was thinking, this nervous idiot again. Our stop, we stand close. Does she hear my heart screaming? Doors open. I am ready, yes, but my voice isn't. She goes her way.

"Goodbye again," I whisper.

Acknowledgements

This book would not exist without the endless support of my beautiful family. Therefore, I would like to start by thanking my husband- Wilian, for supporting me unconditionally in all my projects and crazy dreams. To my children- Kiara and Jayden (Mis amores), for being proud of Mami for writing a book. Such satisfaction was the key to never quitting.

I am also grateful to Noelia Rufete Merlos for motivating and encouraging me to complete this book. I am pleased to share this new journey upon which we both embarked, uniting us again. I wish you the best of luck with your new projects.

Thanks to Camilla Schmid for inspiring me. Your classes uplifted me to start writing.

To James Pearce for not refusing to read my drafts, and sorry to put you through all that.

I would also like to thank the people who have made it possible for this book to reach its final stages; To my most helpful beta readers- Elena Tur Zapata, Kelly-Ann Carr Alves, Mary Zickmund Dusablon, Jadi Blades, Emma Hunt, Wendy Martyn, and Nikki Nunn.

My dedicated editor - Tehreem K, working with you has been a delight.

Finally, but not least, the talented cover designer- Ritiele Ramonica and book designer Hamza.

Thank you all for making my delirious idea come true.

About the Author

Maria D. Lopez Berna was born in Elche - Alicante, Spain. She lives with her husband and two children in Essex, England. She has worked as a language teacher in Spain, Brazil, and England. A lover of literature and passionate about thrillers. Fond of crafts, travelling, drawing, movies, and dancing. A restless soul who enjoys unravelling with words the tales her mind creates.